For Marco

Text and illustration copyright © 2005 by Liane Payne
Design copyright © 2005 by The Templar Company plc

This 2006 edition published by Backpack Books, by arrangement with
The Templar Company plc, Pippbrook Mill, London Road,
Dorking, Surrey, RH4 1JE, UK.

Backpack Books
122 Fifth Avenue
New York, NY 10011

ISBN 0-7607-7186-3

Printed in China

06 07 08 09 MCH 10 9 8 7 6 5 4 3 2 1

Designed by Andy Mansfield
Edited by Sue Harris

a good night bunny book

Bunny and the
Very Windy Day

Liane Payne

BACKPACKBOOKS

NEW YORK

Bunny is very proud of his beautiful garden. He loves tending his flowers, humming and talking to them as he tidies and weeds. But sometimes he says, "I wish I had friends to share my garden with."

One morning, Bunny is woken by a
tap-tap-tapping noise at the window.
He sleepily pulls back the curtain and sees
leaves whirling and swirling outside.
"What a very windy day!" he says.

Bunny hurries outside and finds his beautiful tidy garden all messed up! The wind has whooshed everything round and round—his flowers have flopped over, and his neat little lawn is littered with leaves. "Oh, bother!" says Bunny.

Bunny is very cross with the wind for making such a mess. Sighing, he starts sweeping the leaves into big piles.

He'd soon have his garden looking beautiful and tidy once more—just as it was before the wind ruined it.

But before Bunny can pick up his
neat piles of leaves—WHOOSH!—a huge
gust of wind blows them all away again!
"I don't like the wind," grumbled Bunny.

Bunny was surprised when some little birds sang, "We LOVE the wind! It carried us here to spend the summer in your lovely garden. Then it will help us fly home again before the cold winter comes!"

"Yes, but it still messed up my garden," muttered Bunny, hurrying off to stake up his flowers.

Bunny was still fussing about the wind when a passing butterfly said, "The wind's wonderful. It carries insects to your garden to gather nectar from your splendid flowers!" Bunny smiled. His flowers were splendid, even after all the wind had done!

Bunny was working hard to collect up all the leaves before the wind could blow them away again, when a little voice said, "I like the wind, too. It swirls the leaves into mounds so I can make a cozy nest, and it blows the nuts off the trees for my winter food store!" Bunny looked behind the sack and found a mouse smiling up at him.

"The wind helps you, too, Bunny," continued the mouse. "Look! It's blowing lots of interesting seeds into your garden. Next year, some of them will grow into lovely new plants."

Bunny sat down and began to think. Perhaps the wind wasn't so bad after all. It seemed to be very useful. "In fact," he thought, "the wind has made my wish come true—it's brought me lots of friends to share my garden with!"

That night, Bunny and his new friend, Mouse, were tucked up in Bunny's cozy sitting room as the wind whistled and whooshed outside. Bunny smiled. "I like the wind," he said sleepily. Mouse nodded. "Me, too. It's a shame about the laundry though...."

"Good night, Bunny!"